Horseshoes
#4

Pony Club
RIDER

Pony Club
RIDER

Written by Patricia Leitch

HarperTrophy
A Division of HarperCollinsPublishers

First published in Great Britain by Lions, an imprint of
HarperCollins Publishers, in 1993.

PONY CLUB RIDER
Copyright © 1993 by Patricia Leitch
For information address HarperCollins Children's Books,
a division of HarperCollins Publishers,
10 East 53rd Street, New York, NY 10022.

Library of Congress Cataloging-in-Publication Data
Leitch, Patricia.
    Pony Club rider / written by Patricia Leitch.
        p.   cm. — (Horseshoes ; #4)
    Summary: Ten-year-old friends Sally and Thalia finally make the
Pony Club team but worry about being good enough to compete in
the big One Day Event in October.
    ISBN 0-06-027286-4 (lib. bdg.) — ISBN 0-06-440637-7 (pbk.)
    [1. Horses—Fiction.   2. Horse shows—Fiction.   3. Scotland—
Fiction.]   I. Title.   II. Series: Leitch, Patricia.   Horseshoes ; #4.
PZ7.L5372Po   1996   96-3824
[Fic]—dc20   CIP
                                                                    AC

Typography by Darcy Soper
1   2   3   4   5   6   7   8   9   10
❖
First Edition

This series is for Meg

Don't miss the other books in the
Horseshoes series

Horseshoes #1
THE PERFECT HORSE

Horseshoes #2
JUMPING LESSONS

Horseshoes #3
CROSS-COUNTRY GALLOP

Horseshoes
#4

Pony Club
RIDER

Chapter One

Sally Lorimer and Thalia ("rhymes-with-dahlia-which-is-a-flower-like-a-chrysanthemum") Nesbit sat in the back of Mr. Lorimer's car as he drove them through the gray light of an early autumn evening. Meg, the Lorimers' elderly Bearded collie, sat in the front bracing her feet against the seat as Mr. Lorimer swung the car around the swerves and bends of the country road.

They were going to Ashdale, where Mrs. Blair lived. She was the district commissioner of the Tarentshire branch of the Pony Club. Tonight she was holding a branch meeting to decide who would be on the Tarent Pony Club team for the Pony Club Junior One-Day Event in October.

Sally and Thalia were too tense with excitement and nerves even to speak to each other. In two hours they would know. The team would have been chosen.

"I haven't got a chance," Sally told herself. "Mrs. Blair would never choose me." She groaned aloud in suspense.

Both Sally and Thalia were ten years old. Sally was medium size, with thick brown bangs, and hair that fell straight to her shoulders. Her blue eyes were wide set, and her mouth turned up at the corners, as if she was about to burst out laughing.

Thalia was tall and lean with fizzing, corn-colored hair. She lived with her narg (which is "gran" spelled backward) in a cottage close to the shore. When her parents divorced, they had given Thalia a roan horse called Tarquin. He could gallop faster than gale-blown cloud shadows across the sea. The faster Tarquin galloped, the better Thalia liked it. She rode him effortlessly, sitting tight and neat as Tarquin flew over cross-country obstacles or bright show jumps. Both Mrs. Blair and Martine Dawes, the head instructor at Mr. Frazer's riding school, disapproved of Thalia's wild galloping.

"I bet you they won't pick me because I'm too fast," Thalia said to herself. "But you need a fast horse for cross-country. You need a horse like Tarquin, who isn't afraid of jumping strange obstacles."

The Lorimer family had come to live at Kestrel Manor six months ago. Kestrel Manor was a huge stone house. It was built on its own peninsula of land that jutted out into the sea, joined to the mainland only by a long, broad avenue lined with copper beech trees.

Mr. Lorimer was a librarian. Mrs. Lorimer did her best to be a busy housewife, but she much preferred wandering around looking at things and painting in watercolors and inks. Ben Lorimer was fifteen. He was tall for his age, with a shock of black hair like his father's. He spent most of his time reading. Jamie was the youngest Lorimer. He was four and liked mice. The Lorimers also had two dogs. Meg was a twelve-year-old black-and-white Bearded collie, and Misty, a gray-and-white Beardie, was five.

They had all fallen in love with Kestrel Manor when they first discovered it, empty, neglected, and drowning in an overgrown garden.

Although they had all ached to live at Kestrel Manor, they knew they could never afford to buy it. Then Mr. Lorimer's great-uncle Nathan died in Australia. Mr. Lorimer had hardly known him, but since Great-uncle Nathan had no family of his own, he left Mr. Lorimer a considerable amount of money and at last their dream had come true. They all came to live at Kestrel Manor.

Before she came to Kestrel Manor, Sally had ridden only at Miss Meek's riding school. Up and down, up and down Miss Meek's lane on aged ponies who tripped over their hooves and ignored their riders, while they dreamed of meadows beside slow-flowing rivers where they could roll and graze in freedom.

Sally had met Thalia when her family came around to look at Kestrel Manor before they bought it. Sally's first ride on Tarquin had been a disaster. Tarquin, knowing that Sally was not in control, had galloped madly across the beach, leaped the jetty, then swung around to race back to Thalia with Sally clinging to his mane—a helpless passenger.

But that was before Sally rescued Willow from a meat man. Willow was a dapple-gray mare with a dished Araby face and huge, dark

Arab eyes. Her silver mane lay over her arched neck and her tail fell over strong-boned hocks. She was completely reliable. Gradually Sally had learned to trust her, to gallop and jump. And finally, at last weekend's Tarent Horse Show, she and Willow had been first with Thalia and Tarquin in the cross-country pairs class. Mrs. Blair had been at the show. After seeing them jump, she had asked them both to join the Pony Club and be considered for the Junior One-Day Event team.

"But she won't pick me. I know she won't. She'll only want to borrow Willow for someone else to ride. She'll remember how nervous I was. She'll never pick me," Sally told herself as Mr. Lorimer stopped the car in front of Ashdale. Immediately the front door opened and Mr. Blair was welcoming them in.

"Come in, come in. You are the last. Mr. Lorimer? So good of you to bring them. Where would the Pony Club be without its parents, that's what I say. Now, coffee is laid out for parents. Of course, bring in the old dog too. We'll find a rug for her. Girls, down that way to the study. They're waiting for you."

Before she knocked on the solid-oak door, Thalia swallowed hard. "They must pick us. They must," she swore through clenched teeth.

Sally shuddered, suddenly seeing impossible cross-country obstacles looming in front of her and hearing show jumps crashing down behind her. She shook her head firmly. That was in the past.

"We must be on the team," she vowed. And for that second she didn't think about letting the team down or falling off, only of the magical, glorious moment when the Tarentshire team—including Thalia and herself—were presented with the cup.

"Come in," called Mrs. Blair. Thalia opened the door to a comfortably furnished room lit by table lamps and the flames of a log fire. The gray evening was shut out by heavy velvet curtains. The walls were garlanded with show ribbons. Mrs. Blair was short and thickset, and Martine Dawes was young, dark, and dashing. They sat together on a sofa behind a coffee table covered with Pony Club folders and papers.

"Now, find yourselves a place and I'll let you

all know what we have decided," Mrs. Blair told them.

There were seven other children in the study sitting in the huge armchairs or on cushions on the floor. Sally and Thalia recognized three of the girls and one boy only by sight, but they knew Simon Knowles. Simon was an amazing rider, but after a fall on a cross-country course—in which he had broken both his legs, and his horse Merlin, who also broke a leg, had to be put down—he had refused to jump again. It was not until the Tarent show, when Sally had persuaded Simon's father to buy Clover, one of Miss Meek's riding-school ponies, that Simon had begun to regain his confidence.

Verity Blair, one of Mrs. Blair's daughters, was sitting astride the arm of a sofa. She rode Buster, a solid bay that had been passed down through the family.

Charlotte Main was there. She was one of Thalia's and Sally's least favorite people.

"Bet the pimply Charlotte will be picked," Thalia whispered to Sally. "Ignore her if she comes near us."

"Right," said Mrs. Blair, standing up. "Great

to see you all here. I would love to tell you that you are all candidates for the team, but that cannot be. We have picked six candidates. After the six have been training for a few weeks, Martine and I will pick the four who will make up our team. This year the branch event is at Leighton Hall, on the third Saturday in October. So we have a lot of hard riding to do before then."

"Come on, Mom!" interrupted Verity. "We are all desperate to know who you've chosen."

"I shall put you out of your misery this very second." Mrs. Blair reached for a typewritten list of names. "Martine and I have given a lot of careful consideration to this list. But, remember, for the ones who have not been picked, there is always next year. . . .

"Verity is in. Not because she is my daughter but because we need Buster as our anchor. He has been to several events and he knows what it's all about.

"Simon, I hear you have a new horse?"

"Dad bought her yesterday. She's super." But Simon's face didn't show any enthusiasm.

"We were a bit worried about you. Didn't

think Clover would have the stamina. But with a new horse you're a candidate. You are in."

As she listened, Sally felt the warm room change to arctic winter. If Simon had a new horse, what would happen to Clover? Would his father sell her? Could she end up back at Miss Meek's riding school?

"Third rider," continued Mrs. Blair, "is Charlotte Main. We have chosen you after a lot of thought. If you are repeatedly late for practices, you will not be on the team, no matter how well Pie is jumping. Understood?"

Charlotte scowled but nodded. "I'm the best rider here . . ." she began, but Mrs. Blair ignored her.

"Brian Green," she said to the boy Sally and Thalia didn't know. "How is Punch?"

"Fine," said Brian, pushing his curly brown hair out of his eyes and looking away from Mrs. Blair.

"Then brush him down, wake him up, and bring him along to Saturday's practice."

"Oh, thanks. Thank you," said Brian in an amazed voice.

Only Sally, Thalia, and the three girls they didn't know were left.

"Thalia, you are in. We hope you will see sense and steady Tarquin. We don't want a broken neck, either yours or the horse's. So slow down."

"I will. I promise I will." Thalia beamed, but in her mind's eye she was already galloping Tarquin over drops and ditches at flat-out speed.

Sally dug her nails into the palms of her hands. The three girls she didn't know all looked far more competent than herself. They all looked as if they had been riding for years.

"Last team member . . . Sally, we've chosen you. Martine thinks you have improved tremendously since you've been riding Willow. This is your chance. Keep on improving and you are on the team."

Sally and Thalia beamed at each other. They were both in.

"But of course," said Charlotte to no one in particular, "the trouble will start if she falls off Willow and won't get on again."

Mrs. Blair ignored her, but Sally blushed

scarlet. Before she had Willow, she had fallen off one of Mr. Frazer's horses and refused to get on again. Charlotte had been there. But it had all been months ago. Sally had almost forgotten about it. Only someone as horrible as Charlotte would have mentioned it.

Mrs. Blair spoke briefly about the one-day event, explaining that it was a small branch event, with five teams competing. There would be a simple dressage test, a cross-country course, and then show jumping. They would all have a lot to do before October. The first team practice was at Ashdale next Saturday, one o'clock sharp. Martine would instruct. She looked forward to seeing them all.

"See you tomorrow," Thalia shouted, waving good-bye when Mr. Lorimer had dropped her off at her narg's cottage. "Got to start getting them in shape."

"Sounds like hard work," said Sally's father as he drove off.

"It will be," replied Sally, nodding contentedly. It was beyond all her dreams to have been picked for a Pony Club team. She didn't care how hard she had to work.

Suddenly Sally glimpsed a silver-white shape standing close to the hedge. It was a white greyhound. Caught in the glare of the headlights, it seemed a magical glimmering being. It had long, delicate legs, a tight-muscled body, an arched neck, and a fine-boned head. Any other dog's eyes would have shone red or green in the headlights, but the white hound's eyes gleamed like luminous, rose-colored crystals.

Sally caught her breath at this sudden glimpse of beauty, this gift from the dark.

"Stop!" she shouted. "Look! In the hedge. There's a dog . . ." But her father had no intention of stopping.

Telling her family that she had been chosen as a candidate for the team filled up the rest of Sally's evening. It wasn't until she was sitting on the window seat in her bedroom looking out over the sea that Sally remembered the strange white hound.

Before they bought Kestrel Manor, the Lorimers had been for a picnic in Fintry Bay close by. They were packing up to go home when Sally had wandered down to the sea's edge by herself. She had seen something glinting in the water and had crouched down to find out what it was. As she reached her hand out into the sea, the waves had swept a tiny crystal unicorn into her open palm.

It was just after this that they had heard about Mr. Lorimer's inheritance. Then they had come to live at Kestrel Manor, Sally had made friends with Thalia, and she had found Willow. Sally was sure that it was a magic unicorn. She always kept it in her pocket or standing on her bedroom windowsill, where the sea light danced rainbows around it.

"We're both on the team, at least as candidates," Sally whispered, holding the unicorn in the palm of her hand. It was then that she remembered the silver-white hound that had stood so still as they drove past. There had been a magic about it, too—a calm stillness that echoed in Sally's mind, a silver-rose hound touched with unicorn magic.

Chapter Two

Simon's new horse burst out of the Knowleses' trailer into the stable yard at Ashdale like an exploding space rocket. Simon, clutching at her halter rope, raced beside her.

"There's a horse for you!" roared Mr. Knowles. "That's a horse worth riding. Cost me the best part of two thousand pounds, but worth every penny of it. She'll take Simon back to the top, where he belongs."

Sally and Thalia were already mounted. Martine had brought them to Ashdale in Mr. Frazer's horse trailer for the first team practice.

"Whee!" exclaimed Thalia in total admiration, hardly noticing Tarquin's rearing fright. "What an incredible horse! Not as good as Tarquin, of course," she added, just in case anyone had heard her.

Willow pricked neat, surprised ears and watched the display through mild eyes.

Remembering Simon's terrible fall, Sally wondered how he would cope with such a lightning horse. Only a few days ago Simon had been unwilling to ride Clover at the Tarent show. And now his father had bought him a mad runaway horse to ride.

Sally had called Simon to make sure that they would not sell Clover. Simon had assured her that they would never, ever dream of selling Clover, for it was Clover that had given him back his confidence. She would have a home with them always. But Sally couldn't be sure.

A stupid horse to buy for Simon, she decided. His father must be a bit crazy.

Simon, with no sign of nerves, had jumped into the saddle and was walking the black horse around on a loose rein, speaking quietly to her, giving her time to settle.

"I don't believe it," groaned Martine to Mrs. Blair. "Just when Simon has started riding again, that idiot of a father had to buy him a horse like that!"

Mrs. Blair nodded her head in agreement.

"Everyone," called Martine, clapping her hands to get their attention. "Down to the paddock."

Simon and Thalia led the way on high-trotting horses. Next came Verity, sitting securely on Buster. Sally rode beside her, trying not to look at the cross-country obstacles, which seemed to grow bigger every second. Brian Green rode behind them on a shaggy, ungroomed horse. A handful of parents brought up the rear.

They had been schooling for nearly half an hour when Charlotte, riding her piebald, came trotting full out down to the paddock.

"It was all Mom's fault," she shouted. "I kept telling her to get a move on and then the phone rang and she gossiped for hours."

Martine ignored her. Mrs. Blair looked pointedly at her watch but said nothing.

They schooled for another ten minutes. Then they left their horses with the parents while they walked around eight squashed-down cross-country obstacles. Martine showed them the correct way to take each one.

"I think," said Thalia to Sally, "that if your horse is going fast enough you can clear anything."

"Well, you would, wouldn't you!" snapped

Martine, overhearing Thalia. "But you are *wrong*. I am here to tell you the correct way to ride a cross-country course. Please have the manners to listen."

Thalia did not apologize. When it was her turn to ride, she went around the jumps at a blazing gallop, soaring high and clear over every one.

Willow took Sally around at a careful canter.

"A little more speed?" suggested Mrs. Blair. "Perhaps if you stood next to Thalia you might blend together. Then you could both jump at a medium pace."

Simon struggled to control Zodiac, but her head was up and she charged the jumps, throwing herself over them in a furious fandango of mane, tail, and flying hooves.

"She needs a martingale and no more cross-country," warned Martine. "Cavaletti and trotting in circles until you've balanced her up."

Buster, who knew the course well, popped around with a flick of his tail. Mrs. Blair told her daughter off for not kicking him on.

Punch, Brian Green's pony, trotted up to the first three obstacles and ducked around them.

At the fourth jump—a brush fence—he swung around and belted back to the other horses.

Charlotte rode over the course smoothly and efficiently, her piebald accurately timing his takeoffs and landings. Going at a steady gallop, she made nothing of the small jumps and rode back to the others with a superior expression on her face.

"Well done," said Martine. Turning to Thalia, she added, "That's how Tarquin would jump if you would only let him settle."

"I wouldn't want Tarquin to jump like that. Tarquin cleared them all and he was ten billion times faster than Pie," said Thalia, answering back.

Martine's reply was drowned by Mrs. Blair, who instructed everyone to go over to the show-jumping paddock.

"Let's make it a race," Charlotte challenged as they rode down to the show jumps. "Whoever is fastest is the winner."

"Don't be silly," said Sally. "We're here to practice for the team. The one-day event isn't a speed competition." But she saw Simon grinning and passing on the dare to Thalia.

Simon jumped first. He winked at Charlotte as he rode into the field with its precise arrangement of show jumps. They were to ride over four jumps around the outside of the paddock and then down the center over parallel poles.

Thalia stood up in her stirrups, bright with excitement as she watched Simon and Zodiac race around the outside jumps. Zodiac increased her speed at every jump. By the time she came charging down the center of the paddock, Simon, his face set, was pulling helplessly at his reins. Zodiac slipped as she took off, almost skidded into the poles, then leaped hopelessly high and landed on the middle of the jump. There was a crash of breaking poles and Simon was thrown to the ground as Zodiac, high-stepping as a spider in water, fought to free herself from the wreckage.

For a second everyone seemed to hold their breath. Then Mrs. Blair was running to Simon, shouting at him not to get up. Martine rushed to catch Zodiac.

"Nothing to make a fuss about," shouted Simon's father. "Boy's used to taking a toss."

But for once his usual bossy expression had changed to one of concern.

Sally sat on Willow, watching helplessly. There was nothing she could do. She could only wait to see if Simon would remount and jump again.

Martine checked Zodiac and found nothing wrong with her. Simon scrambled to his feet.

"Nothing broken?" asked Mrs. Blair, making Simon move his arms and legs and wriggle his fingers and toes.

"I'm fine," said Simon, but Sally, watching intently, saw the fear in his eyes and his tucked-in lips. Then he straightened his shoulders and drew in his breath, forcing himself to ride again.

He took Zodiac from Martine, mounted, and cantered her in a circle. Before his father had time to shout, he had turned Zodiac and ridden over the four jumps around the paddock. In spite of her crash Zodiac cleared them easily, and this time Simon managed to control her speed.

"Good boy," praised Mrs. Blair. "Well done. Now, no more jumping until we steady her up. Sitting trot and patience."

"Okay," said Simon, a sudden smile of relief lighting his tense face.

"She's got a good jump in her," said Martine. "I'll come over and help you. We'll soon get her sorted out."

Thalia was next.

"You've seen for yourself what happens when you let a horse tear around out of control," Mrs. Blair told her. For once Thalia had nothing to say.

She nodded, not looking at Mrs. Blair, but still sent Tarquin sailing on over the jumps.

Charlotte had two refusals. She rode back scowling, making Sally think that if Mrs. Blair hadn't been there she would have been using her riding whip in temper.

Buster popped around obligingly, and Brian on Punch had eight refusals.

Sally was still so shaken by Simon's fall that she forgot that this was jumping and she should be feeling nervous. Without thinking about it she sat easily over the jumps, going with her horse.

"Very nice," said Martine. "You have remembered the things I taught you."

"But I wasn't even thinking about what I should be doing," gasped Sally, suddenly feeling guilty.

"That's even better," laughed Martine. "You were doing what came naturally."

It was late afternoon before Sally and Thalia were sitting next to Martine in the horse trailer, driving home to Kestrel Manor. Tarquin and Willow were safely tied in the box behind them.

Mrs. Blair had handed out typed sheets giving each of them details of feeding, exercise, and the dates of future team practices. She told them that they all had a long way to go before they could even begin to think of themselves as a team.

Martine drove quickly through the gathering gray dusk, chatting about past events and the horses she had ridden. They had almost reached the turnoff for Kestrel Manor when Martine jammed her foot on the brake, bringing the horse trailer to a violent halt.

"Glory be!" she shouted as she threw herself out of the cabin. "Never saw it. Another second and I'd have been over it!"

Sally and Thalia scrambled out with her.

"What?" demanded Thalia. "What was it?"

"Dog," said Martine. "Big white dog. Don't know how I missed it. It ran straight in front of me."

"There it is!" cried Sally. She pointed to where the white hound was standing on the other side of the road. It was the hound she had glimpsed from her father's car.

The hound stood perfectly still. Her delicate bones, long fragile-seeming legs, sickle tail, sweet reach of neck, and delicate head gave her a strange beauty. She watched them through her pale eyes as they crossed the road toward her.

"That was close! She's invisible in this light," said Martine.

Sally reached out her hand to stroke the hound, but hesitated. Somehow it seemed wrong to touch her. She wasn't that kind of dog. Unlike the Beardies, who leaped and bounced over everyone they met, the white hound had a cool distance about her, a center of silence that made Sally draw back.

Two men burst through the hedge behind the horse trailer. They were both roughly dressed in muddied boots and worn jackets.

"Here, you!" one of them shouted. "Leave the dog alone. Don't you go petting a dog like that one. Wait till I get her."

He knotted the dirty rope he was carrying around the hound's neck.

"You keep your hands off of it," he said.

"You should have had her on a leash," Martine told them sharply. "You're lucky I didn't run her over. No dog should be running loose like that."

The man grunted and yanked at the rope. Dragging the white hound behind him, he and his companion walked off, away from Kestrel Manor. The white hound's movements were filled with grace as she trotted beside the shambling humans.

"She can't belong to them," cried Sally, watching them go.

"But she does," said Thalia. "They're staying in the cottage at Mr. Palmer's farm, working for him. She's their dog."

"They don't deserve to have a dog like that," said Sally bitterly. "They must have stolen her from somewhere."

Mrs. Lorimer and Ben had put down beds for the horses, who were in at night now, then filled hay nets and water buckets. When the horses were settled and eating their feed, Martine came back to Kestrel Manor for coffee.

"Narg's here," Mrs. Lorimer told Thalia, who followed them across the grass to the house.

Sally waited for a moment to watch Willow eating her feed. She loved to see her secure and settled for the night.

"You were the best horse," Sally told her before she swung away to race after the others.

She had almost caught up with them when she saw that Misty was leaping around Martine, but there was no sign of Meg. Sally looked back and saw Meg making her way slowly toward her.

"Well, come on," Sally cried. "Did we leave you behind?"

Meg trotted a few stiff steps, then fell back into a walk.

"It's all right. I'm waiting for you," Sally told her.

As she stood silently in the gathering dark, she put her hand into her jacket pocket,

cradling the crystal unicorn. With her dream-
ing eye she saw the unicorn stepping between
the dark gold and pearl of silver birch trees, the
white hound by its side.

Chapter Three

September settled into solid rain. Fields were flooded, and the gateway to the horses' field was churned into a swamp of mud.

Martine came out to Kestrel Manor and trace-clipped Willow and Tarquin.

"I haven't taken too much off," she said when she finished. "Just under their stomachs and chests."

"Please, please, couldn't you clip all of Tarquin? He would look like a racehorse, a Thoroughbred. I've always longed to see him clipped out and spiffed up. Please?"

"You'll have enough to do coping with New Zealand rugs—filthy, muddy, soaking wet New Zealand rugs—but they do mean that your horses can go out during the day. You don't have to exercise them if the weather is too appalling."

"Oh, but we will exercise them," said Sally. "Mrs. Blair's instructions say that we have to exercise every day, road work at a walk and sitting trot."

"Good for you," said Martine. "Wish I had your energy."

In the mornings and after school Sally and Thalia rode through the rain.

"We need goggles with windshield wipers," Sally said as she kicked Willow on into the deluge.

"Umbrella hats," said Thalia, sitting tightly on Tarquin as he reared trying to escape from the driving rain and gallop back to Kestrel Manor.

Mr. Lorimer had persuaded Thalia's narg to let him pay for Tarquin's feeding and anything else that Thalia or her horse might need.

"A good thing she agreed," said Thalia. "No way could we ever have afforded all this feeding and rugs. Your father is my fairy godfather."

"Perhaps your parents would have paid something?" suggested Sally.

"My dad can hardly afford a birthday card," said Thalia. "I get all knotted up in case my father appears and wants to take Tarquin away and sell him."

"He couldn't do that!" exclaimed Sally.

"J-O-K-E joke," said Thalia, but Sally thought that it wasn't completely a joke.

One Saturday was so wet that Mrs. Blair phoned them to tell them to leave their horses at home and bring only themselves to Ashdale. When they were all sitting around the table in Mrs. Blair's study, she gave out cards for them to keep with a diagram of the dressage arena and details of the dressage test for the Junior Event. They would begin by saluting the judge from the middle of the arena and then had to ride different movements, stopping and starting at the different letters marked outside the arena.

"It is quite simple," said Mrs. Blair. "Remember that."

"When can we practice it?" asked Charlotte, who had arrived late and was making up for it by asking bossy questions.

"Never," said Mrs. Blair. "We will ride all the different figures in the test but not in the correct order. You will ride it only once before the event. If you ride the test only a few times, your horse begins to know what he has to do next. It's called anticipating, and it's a real no-no! So walk the test on your feet, walk it with your fingers around a table, and ride it in your mind every spare second. You must wear gloves when you are riding the test. When you salute the judge, you have your reins in one hand, your other hand is down by your side, and you salute by nodding your head."

"The dressage is the worst," said Martine as she drove them home. "I love the cross-country and the show jumping, but the dressage—ugh! When I ride into the arena all on my own, my mind just fudges up. I cannot remember a thing. Have no idea where to go."

"Tarquin won't like it," said Thalia. "He hates schooling."

"Or *you* do?" suggested Martine.

Sally was sure Willow would enjoy dressage. Walking, trotting, and cantering at the correct letters placed around the arena, being neat and accurate. "And," thought Sally, "nothing to be afraid of."

But she pushed the thought out of her head. That didn't matter now. She was not afraid.

That evening Sally and Ben went down to say good night to the horses. Misty was in the kitchen helping Mr. Lorimer clean up by gulping down the scraps before he washed the plates. But Meg came with them, getting out of her basket in a stiff, bumbling hurry, her face anxious in case she was going to be left behind.

Tarquin was still pulling at strands of hay caught in his hay net while Willow lay like a cuddly toy snug in her bed of deep straw. Even when Sally and Ben looked in over her half door, she didn't get to her feet.

"So lucky," said Sally, her spine shivering with delight as she laid her arms along the stall door and rested her chin on her arms. "A horse of my own, Thalia and Tarquin, and living here."

"And being on the Pony Club team," added Ben, half teasing, half agreeing.

"I might not be," said Sally. "Mrs. Blair still has to pick *the* team. Two of us will be dropped. Only four in the real team. Mrs. Blair is telling us next week."

"What will you do if Thalia gets picked and you don't?"

"Die," said Sally, shrugging the possibility away from her. It was an idea so terrible that she didn't dare to think about it.

They went back across the stable yard. Meg had not come with them to the stables but was sitting in the grass panting as she waited for them. As they reached her she got to her feet and followed behind them, her head lifted, following their smell.

"Come on, Meg," Sally shouted, pausing to let Meg catch up with them. "You're a lazy old dog."

Meg broke into a trot, her white, paddy paws flopping up and down.

"That's it," encouraged Sally. But just then Meg stopped suddenly. She stood for a moment gasping for breath, then fell over on her side and lay still.

"Meg!" Sally screamed as she dashed to her. "Ben, there's something wrong with Meg!"

Meg's eyes were closed and her breathing was harsh. When Sally crouched down beside her, stroking her, she took no notice but lay stretched out in the long grass without moving.

Ben ran for their father while Sally waited, stroking Meg's dense hair and holding her limp paws.

"She just fell down," Sally said when Mr. Lorimer came racing toward them. "She's not dead, is she? She's not dead?"

"Of course not," said Mr. Lorimer sharply. "Don't know if we should try and move her or not. Ben, phone for the vet."

"Right," Ben said, and raced back to the house.

"We have to do something," pleaded Sally desperately, tears running down her cheeks. "We can't leave her lying here."

"I don't know. Perhaps . . ." began Mr. Lorimer. Even as he spoke, Meg gave a sudden shudder and lifted her head.

She looked around with a dazed expression, then stood up, her tail wagging. She took a few steps away from them, then looked around again, barking to know why they were all standing there instead of getting home to the fire.

"She's better!" Sally exclaimed. "Maybe she only needed a nap."

"It's a bit more than that, I'm afraid," said Mr. Lorimer. "We'll see what the vet has to say."

Sally reached out for her father's hand and held on to it tightly. Although Meg was walking ahead of them, Sally knew there was something wrong. Meg had not just been asleep.

Dr. Cheever, the vet, arrived about an hour later. He examined Meg, taking her temperature, looking at her eyes and mouth, and listening to her heart.

"She's okay now," he said, giving Meg a last pat before he stood up. "May never happen again. How old is she?"

"Twelve," said Mr. Lorimer.

"Fair age," said Dr. Cheever.

"It's not!" cried Sally. "It's not very old at all."

Her mother drew Sally to her side, hugging her close while they listened to the vet.

"Maybe you're right," he said to Sally. "She could go on for years. It's her heart. Bit tired. Something went wrong for a second when she keeled over. I'll give her an injection, and could someone pick up pills for her tomorrow? There's a good chance you'll never notice anything wrong again. Bring her in to see me in a month."

Sally went slowly up to her room. She did not want Meg to be old. She did not want her to be ill. No matter what the vet said, if it was Meg's heart, it must be serious.

Through her window Sally could see the swell and glint of the sea. The moon threw black shadows and struck a silver radiance from the crystal unicorn standing in its place on the windowsill. Sally stood staring at the unicorn, hardly seeing it, thinking only about Meg. Then a movement outside caught her gaze. Looking through the glass, she saw the white hound crossing the lawn.

The hound paused and looked straight at Sally. For a second she stood with her front paw lifted, her sickle tail carving the dark and her strange pale eyes looking up from her porcelain-fine head. Almost before Sally could be sure she was there, she had turned and vanished into the shadows.

Chapter Four

"**O**f course you didn't see it," said Thalia as they were setting out next Monday morning to exercise. "It was your imagination. Honestly, those men have been gone for ages. The cottage is all locked up."

"Well, the hound is still here. I did see her."

Thalia looked at her watch. "We've just got time before school to ride around by the cottage. Then you can see for yourself. Okay?"

Before Sally had a chance to disagree, Thalia led the way down the trail from Kestrel Manor to the shore.

When the horses felt the sand beneath their hooves, they were filled with a longing for speed. Tarquin pranced excitedly by the wave crests and gleaming sands, and Willow clinked her bit and gathered herself together. At exactly the same moment they charged forward.

Sally sat easily as Willow cantered along. Clouds of raucous gulls rose in front of them, wheeling overhead, then settling again precisely above their reflections once the horses had passed.

Too much, thought Sally. Too much is happening.

She was sure, absolutely certain, that she had seen the white hound. As certain as she was that Mrs. Lee, her teacher, was going to be very annoyed with the messy project Sally had handed in last week. She had rushed through it so she would have more time to ride.

Next Saturday was only five days away. Then she would know if she had been picked for the team or not. Too much. Too much.

And then there was Meg. The thought of Meg being ill swept over Sally like a thundercloud. Nothing must happen to Meg. She must always be there. They wouldn't be a real family without Meg.

"Hurry up," commanded Thalia, "or we're going to be late for school."

Sally eased her reins, letting Willow gallop on, leaving behind the fear of Meg dying and the dread of Thalia being picked for the team without her.

They rode up past Narg's and along a trail to the farmer's cottage.

"See," said Thalia. "Absolutely shut. The men have been away for weeks."

Seeing the padlocked door and the windows shuttered against the winter gales, Sally couldn't argue.

"But who is looking after the hound?" she demanded.

"I expect they took her with them. Must have been another dog you saw," said Thalia, turning Tarquin and trotting him toward the road.

Mrs. Lorimer was waiting for them at the stables.

"Where have you been?" she said crossly. "Put your horses into the stalls and I'll see to them. Your father's waiting for you. For goodness sake, get a move on or he'll have to go without you."

"We had to find out about something. Something really urgent," explained Thalia. "We didn't realize it was so late."

"Thalia, get a move on!" roared Mrs. Lorimer, losing her temper. Thalia abandoned

Tarquin and raced for Kestrel Manor, where she had left her school clothes earlier that morning.

Mrs. Lee was not willing to listen to Sally's excuses about her sloppy project on British trees. Mrs. Lee thought homework should come before riding and told Sally so, while Sally stood, not hearing a word she said. She was too worried about the white hound. Who would take care of her now that the men had gone?

"I want the whole thing done again and handed in next Monday morning."

"By then," Sally thought, "we will know who is on the team. It will all be settled." She took her project from Mrs. Lee, hardly glancing at it.

The next Saturday Sally and Thalia, holding their horses, stood in the stable yard waiting for Martine to arrive with the horse trailer. Although Mrs. Blair had told them that she would be picking the team today, that was all she had said. Sally stood leaning against Willow's saddle, going over and over the dressage test. Thalia, who hadn't thought too much about the dressage test, was imagining Tarquin soaring over Mrs. Blair's show jumps.

"Do you think Mrs. Blair will have a competition and the first four will be the team?" Sally asked.

"Nope," said Thalia. "They will have made up their minds by now. They won't have chosen Punch. Bound to choose Buster and the loathsome, pimply Charlotte. That leaves Simon, you, and me. Two of us on the team. One not."

Thalia's voice went squeaky and she looked away from Sally, staring up the drive, willing the horse trailer to appear.

"Tarquin must be on the team," she thought. "*Must* be. And Sally. It wouldn't be any good without Sally."

The horse trailer came clattering down the drive. They loaded their horses and climbed up into the cabin.

"Don't look at me like that," Martine told them. "I don't know who is going to be on the team."

Even when they arrived at Ashdale, there was no mention of choosing the team. They schooled and then took turns walking, trotting, and cantering in a circle, changing reins and circling again in the opposite direction at the different paces.

Charlotte was so late that she hardly had time to school at all. She came galloping into the paddock, her hard hat stuck on the back of her head, her jacket unbuttoned.

"Hope I haven't missed anything," she yelled. "Not much point in schooling Pie. He knows it all."

If Mrs. Blair heard, she said nothing.

When Charlotte had ridden her circles, they went for a ride over the hill with Martine riding Mr. Blair's gray hunter.

"En-joy, en-joy," Thalia whispered to Sally. "We've got all this land to ride in, terrific horses, and you jumped that drop without shifting an inch."

"Enjoy myself!" said Simon, overhearing. "Some hope. Zodiac goes bonkers when she gallops, and my father will murder me if I'm not on the team. Why hasn't she told us?"

But Sally and Thalia had no time to answer. Martine was trotting on downhill, checking up on them over her shoulder.

Like a pied piper Martine rode ahead of them. They followed where she led—popping over dry stone walls, twisting suddenly to jump a ditch, then galloping on over rough moorland. They finished with a long canter, jumping over a pole propped up by a rusty bulk of farm machinery, then slowing to a trot as they swung around the side of the hill.

"That blew the cobwebs away!" said Martine, grinning. She stood up in her stirrups and checked over horses and riders.

"Oh, again, again," cried Thalia. "That was super!"

They cooled their horses off by walking them back to Ashdale along the road. When they reached the yard, there was no sign of Mrs. Blair. Martine told everyone to stable their horses because Mrs. Blair wanted to see them, minus muddy boots, for a few minutes in her study.

"This is it," groaned Simon.

"I just hope she doesn't keep us too long," grumbled Charlotte. "I don't see why I should have to wait. Pie is bound to be on the team. I think she should just tell me and let me go."

"Right," said Mrs. Blair when they had all

found a place to sit. "This is what you have all been waiting for."

"Please," thought Sally desperately. "Please pick me."

"You've all done very well, but as you know the team has to consist of four riders, so two of you must go. It wouldn't be fair to you or your horses to expect you to come to team practices when I know you are not going to be on the team.

"Brian, I'm sorry, but Punch is not fast enough. It would take a stronger rider than you to wake him up, so I'm afraid you are out."

"That's okay, Mrs. Blair," said Brian cheerfully. "I'd rather go to rugby with my dad."

"Verity is in. We need Buster to hold us together."

"Simon, you are in. Let's hope you can come to terms with Zodiac before the event. At present you both have potential."

"Whew! Thank goodness," said Simon. "My old man would have blown a gasket if you'd dropped us."

"Which leaves us with Charlotte, Thalia, and Sally. One of you has got to go."

Mrs. Blair paused, and the silence in the room was so loud they could all hear it.

"Well, I've decided to keep Thalia on the team."

Thalia gave a gulp of delight, and Sally dug her nails even deeper into the palms of her hands.

"But you must steady Tarquin. You are perfectly capable of slowing him down if you want to. Understood?"

Thalia nodded vigorously.

"Now, Charlotte or Sally? Charlotte has been riding a good bit longer than Sally and she has done some competition riding."

Charlotte's face beamed smugly.

"Of course I knew . . ." she began to say to Verity.

"But she has been late for every practice," continued Mrs. Blair. "Not the fault of her ride—I've checked with her mother. She has paid next to no attention to Martine's instruction. She has continued to chat when she has been repeatedly told to be quiet. In fact she has been an intolerable nuisance for most of the time."

Charlotte's mouth dropped open. She stared furiously at Mrs. Blair.

"Sally, on the other hand, has worked and improved both her own riding and her horse. We don't know—perhaps Willow has already been ridden in a one-day event. But we shall see how she goes in October. I've decided to make Sally the fourth member of the team."

"But that's not fair," stormed Charlotte. "I'm a far better rider than Sally. She's so nervous."

"That's quite enough," warned Mrs. Blair. "Charlotte and Brian, thank you both for coming. I hope you won't think it has been time wasted. Now, I'd like the team to stay on for another minute or two."

Charlotte stamped out. Brian thanked Mrs. Blair before he left.

"You are *the* team," Mrs. Blair said when they had gone. "For the one-day event the three top scores will count. That means should any-thing disastrous happen to one of you, the other three *must* complete all three parts of the event or the team is eliminated."

Instantly Sally imagined messing up the dressage, falling off on the cross-country, and knocking everything down in the show jumping.

"As well as the team cup there is a cup for the best individual. I expect you to win them both!"

"Naturally," said Thalia.

"One last thing before you go. A week from next Saturday, that's in a fortnight, we are going to have a mini one-day event here at Ashdale. I've invited the Haxton Pony Club over for the day. We will ride *the* dressage test, go around some of the cross-country obstacles that your horses don't know, and finish up with show jumping. The real thing. Ribbons for the winners."

"Super!" rejoiced Thalia. "Tarquin will love it."

Simon said nothing. He looked down at his hands spread out on his knees. The Pony Club Junior One-Day Event would have been the first cross-country competition he had ridden in since his fall on Merlin. A bit of Simon was still terrified. He could still hear the thud as Merlin's hind legs hit the fixed poles, feel Merlin's bulk on top of him and the pain in his own legs. He had been counting the days to the

Pony Club Event, building up his courage. Now, in just two short weeks, he was to be part of a team again, riding fast over fixed jumps because he couldn't let the team down.

Sally didn't know what to think, whether to be glad to have the chance of riding in a competition before the real thing, or to be shivering at the thought.

"You never told me!" cried Verity. "Oh, Mom, why did you choose the Haxton Branch? Why? Why didn't you ask the Penfrew Branch?"

"What are the Haxton Branch like?" Thalia asked Verity.

"Wait and see," said Verity darkly. "You'll know soon enough."

Chapter Five

*I*t was a bright blue, frosty morning, making Sally's toes tingle as she stamped her feet in Ashdale's stable yard and waited for the arrival of the Haxton Pony Club team.

"I wish they'd come," said Verity. "Then we could get mounted. Trust my mother to make us into a welcoming committee."

"Wish I was on Zodiac," Simon agreed. "I feel stupid standing here like this."

Sally stared about her at all the excitement and bustle. The dressage arena was marked out with white letters.

"Enter at A, trot to X, halt, salute judge, remembering to smile. Walk on to C and turn right . . ." Sally repeated under her breath. She knew the test as well as she knew her two times table.

Parents and friends who were there to help with the organization walked about with clipboards, stopwatches, and pens, asking each other if they knew what to do. Narg, Mrs.

Lorimer, and Jamie were setting up a food center in the back of an open horse trailer.

"Oh, hurry up!" demanded Thalia. "Tarquin will be in a filthy mood being dumped in a stall he doesn't know. *Come now!*"

And in answer to Thalia's command a horse trailer came roaring up the drive. It was very new. Its chromework shone, its green enamel gleamed, and painted on its side was a horse's head and the words: HAXTON PONY CLUB.

It stopped smoothly and a woman sprang down from the cabin looking as expensive and newly painted as the trailer itself.

"Hi-i-i," she called. "Wonderful to be here! We're all absolutely dying to meet you. Wonderful day!"

When the horses were led out of the trailer they, too, were bright and gleaming. The two grays, a bay, and a skewbald were all fully clipped out, rugged, and bandaged for the journey in vivid yellows and reds. Their tack was clearly the best.

The two boys who led out the gray horses, a redheaded girl who led out the bay, and a pale girl who had the skewbald all looked as if they had stepped out of advertisements for riding clothes in a horse magazine.

"Hi," they called, waving vaguely in the direction of the Tarent team. "Hi."

But they didn't really see Sally or Thalia or Simon.

"Is there a cup?" one of the boys asked Simon. "We couldn't find out, and one does like to know what one is riding for."

Two slinky cars purred into the yard. The doors opened, and Haxton parents filled the yard with noise.

"My dad would get along with them," said Simon. "They could all shout together."

"I'm going to get Tarquin," Thalia announced, seeing Mrs. Blair and Martine hurrying across the yard toward them. She turned her back on the fuss and bother of the Haxton team.

Although Sally and Verity hung about a little longer, the Haxton team did not seem to need any welcoming. Once mounted on their hard, fit horses, they only wanted to get started.

"Mom, where can we ride them in?"

"Darling, I just do not know. Oh, here's Tilly Blair. She's the one to ask. Hi-i-i! Wonderful to be here. We're all so excited. Now could you tell us . . ."

Sally and Thalia rode down to the field beyond the dressage arena.

"Snobs," said Thalia in disgust.

"They look to me," said Sally, "as if they are going to be excellent riders as well."

The two Haxton boys rode first in the dressage test. They each performed smooth, correct tests and rode out of the arena looking pleased with themselves.

Thalia was next. Sally watched in dismay as Tarquin refused to stand still while Thalia saluted the judge and then scorched his way through the test—trotting when he should have been walking, cantering when he should have been trotting, and where he should have been cantering, bursting into a full-out gallop.

Sally was next. She walked Willow into the arena, with the test perfectly clear in her mind, feeling her horse obedient and supple, paying attention to her. She stopped in front of the judge's Land Rover, felt Willow stand four-square, head balanced, ears listening.

"Remember to smile," Sally thought as she

took her reins into one hand. Her hand was bare when she should have been wearing gloves! Sally's heart thumped in her throat. Mrs. Blair had told them so often that they must wear gloves for the dressage test, and she had forgotten them.

Panic filled her. Was she already eliminated for not wearing gloves? Should she ride out of the arena or go on with the test? For moments she sat on Willow, her mind totally blank, not knowing what to do next.

Then she turned Willow and rode to the end of the arena. She could think of nothing except the terrible fact that she was not wearing gloves and everyone was staring at her. After minutes of muddled riding, she found herself back in front of the judge's Land Rover. In an embarrassed attempt to hide her gloveless hands, she urged Willow straight out of the arena.

"What went wrong?" yelled Thalia. "You messed it up! I thought you knew it."

"I do," muttered Sally, biting her bottom lip to keep herself from crying, knowing that she would be eliminated.

It was another disaster in a day when everything went wrong for the Tarent team.

Although they had all walked the cross-country course with Martine, Thalia lost her way. She missed out a bank and was eliminated for taking the wrong course. Simon fell off at the ditch and did not complete the course.

After her elimination in the dressage, Sally was allowed to go on taking part without competing. She rode Willow over brush fences, barrels, ditches, a wall with an enormous drop, log piles, and a bench, all obstacles that Willow had not jumped before. She had two refusals, which were both her fault, about six grabs at Willow's mane, and a total collapse onto Willow's neck when she landed after the drop.

Only Buster took his rider around successfully, losing time points but finishing safely at his solid canter.

In the show jumping in the afternoon Tarquin cleared all the jumps in high, soaring leaps, with Thalia crouched over his withers like a jockey. At every jump Sally was left behind. She clung on to Willow's mane as if she could not

jump at all. But she did not care. She only
wanted to stay in the saddle. She had given up.

Simon had three refusals at the first jump
and was eliminated.

"Zodiac would have jumped that," said
Thalia. "I think Simon stopped him."

The Haxton team seemed to Sally to have no
faults at all. They all had good scores over the
cross-country. In the show jumping their well-
schooled horses jumped perfectly controlled
rounds, and they rode out again to the applause
of cheering relatives.

"Well done! Well jumped! Good show," cried
their parents in loud, empty voices.

Mrs. Blair presented the ribbons to the Haxton
team, thanked them for coming, and added that
she was sorry the Tarent team had not been able
to offer them a little more competition.

Sally heard Mrs. Blair's voice without listening to it. She only wanted to go home, to be
sitting at the kitchen fire with Meg and Misty
beside her.

Mrs. Lorimer, Jamie, and Narg packed up
and drove away. The Haxton team stabled
their horses and were driven away, shouting,

"Bye-e-e-e, bye-e-e-e," their farewells streaming behind them in loud banners of noise.

"Better find Martine," said Thalia in a flat, defeated voice.

Sally nodded, and they walked their horses across toward the horse trailer.

"You're supposed to put your horses in the stalls they were in this morning," Verity shouted, running across the yard. "Mom wants to have a word with us." Verity grasped her throat in both hands and twisted her face into mock strangulation.

"Not surprising," said Charlotte, walking past with her mother. "Considering the team she chose."

Thalia sprang around, ready to tell Charlotte what she thought of her but could find nothing to say. It had been a dismal downer of a day.

As Sally took off Willow's tack, a woman she didn't know looked in over the half door.

"You're the girl from Kestrel Manor, aren't you?" she asked. "I've been trying to speak to your mother all day, but I kept missing her."

"She's gone home," said Sally, wanting the woman to go away.

"Drat! Perhaps you can help. I live at Fintry Bay and we're being plagued by this stray dog. A sort of white greyhound. Great brute of a thing. And now it's started to attack children. We've been in contact with the dogcatcher, of course. But so far he hasn't managed to catch it. Someone suggested it might be hiding out around Kestrel Manor. Have you seen it?"

Sally stared at the woman; at her stupid doughy face painted like a clown's, blue-tinted white hair, the lumps of metal hanging down from holes in her ears, and her scarlet nails gripping the stall door.

"What do you mean, dangerous? She's not dangerous. She's beautiful. She's the most beautiful dog I've ever seen."

"So you have seen it? It's been annoying you as well? No one's safe with a mad dog like that on the loose. I'm going to let the dog-catcher know that it's been hanging around Kestrel Manor."

Sally stood in the tack room with Thalia, Verity, and Simon while Mrs. Blair told them what she thought of their performance.

"You would think," she said, "that you had done no schooling, no show jumping, and had never jumped a cross-country obstacle in your life. Simon and Thalia, your horses were totally out of control. I was ashamed of you. There may be some excuse for Simon but none for you, Thalia. You still seem to think it is clever to show off on a horse that could break your neck, going on the way Tarquin does. I had hoped that being on the team would give you a more responsible attitude, but there was no sign of it today."

"Yes, but . . ." Thalia began. Mrs. Blair totally ignored her.

"And Sally, what went wrong with you? It wasn't Willow, it was you. I thought that you at least would have learned the dressage test."

But Sally could only think about the silver-white hound. She just could not believe it might be dangerous. She remembered the dog's calm, gentle face and beautiful eyes. Before Sally could believe the ugly rumors, she would have to find out more about what had actually happened. Sally thought the woman had looked as if she would call out a spidercatcher if she found the tiniest spider in her bathroom. She wished desperately that she had not told the woman that she had seen the hound.

"So I shall see you all next Saturday, as usual. Only two weeks until the Event. Though it seems to me there's no point in going on if you can't do better than this."

Martine drove them home to Kestrel Manor in silence. Even Thalia had nothing to say.

They settled their horses, and Thalia went straight home to Narg. Sally walked slowly home to Kestrel Manor, searching the undergrowth for any sign of the white hound. She opened the door, walked into the bright kitchen, and knew instantly that something was wrong.

Meg was lying in front of the fire, stretched out as flat and as empty as an old coat.

"Meg!" cried Sally.

"She's all right," said Mrs. Lorimer, speaking too quickly, too anxiously, letting Sally know that Meg was not all right.

"She had another heart attack this afternoon. Dad got the vet and he's increased her pills. He says she'll be all right. We're to let her take it easy for the next few days."

"Is she going to get better?" demanded Sally. "She is, isn't she?"

But no one answered her.

"The vet's done everything he can," said Mr. Lorimer. "But we've got to remember that she's an old dog."

Chapter Six

T he vet came back on Monday evening.
"Just to check up on her," he said as he
crouched down to speak to Meg.

Sally stood watching, her hands clenched.
She felt as if she were trapped in a tunnel, with
Meg and the vet at one end, and herself at the
other. There was nobody else in the whole
world; only herself standing spellbound as the
vet took out his stethoscope and listened to the
beat of Meg's heart. Sally watched his face,
intent on listening to this all-important heart-
beat that only he could hear.

At last he stood up.

"Sound's okay," he said. "She's holding her
own. I'll give her another injection."

But to Sally it was nowhere near enough.
She wanted the vet to say that Meg was completely better, that she was her young self again.

"Call me if you need me. I've got a beeper,"
the vet told them. "Anyway, I'll drop in again on
Friday. Not sure what time, but I'll fit you in."

Friday was a school holiday.

"Let's work hard," said Thalia, riding Tarquin down to the shore.

"Yes," said Sally. The shame of doing so badly against the Haxton team still shadowed her mind.

For the next half hour they concentrated on their riding. They made their horses walk out with long, balanced strides, circled at a sitting trot, and cantered at a steady, smooth pace.

"I think Tarquin's had enough," Thalia finally shouted, and Sally agreed, slowing Willow to a walk. She patted her hard, fit neck and told her she was the best horse in Tarentshire.

"Let's do some jumping," said Thalia.

"The field is pure mud," said Sally. She felt a cold clutch in her stomach as she remembered how badly she had been left behind when she had jumped on Saturday. "We'd only churn it up more."

"One turn each won't make any difference." Thalia was already turning Tarquin toward Kestrel Manor.

They rode across the horses' field to where the jumps were standing, abandoned for the winter.

"Hold his reins and I'll straighten them out a bit," said Thalia, jumping down from Tarquin.

Sally sat watching as Thalia struggled to set up four jumps in the muddy field. She did not want to jump. She felt cold and nervous, wanting to make up excuses about why she couldn't jump.

"Don't start that again," warned the voice in her head. "You are on the Pony Club team now. Of course you want to jump."

"There," said Thalia. "How's that? Those four?"

Sally eyed the motley collection of poles, boxes, and oil drums that Thalia had set up. They seemed so high that no one in her right mind would think of jumping them.

She opened her mouth to say that she wasn't going to jump, that it was too muddy, that Willow might slip. Then she saw Thalia watching her with a fixed stare and heard herself saying, "I'll go first."

Tight and cold, Sally rode Willow in a circle and let her canter on at the first jump.

Willow pricked her ears and popped over the jump, timing it perfectly. Sally sat neat and still, going with her horse. She landed securely balanced, ready to ride on at the next jump. Her fear had vanished. Totally, completely, as if it had never been.

"For I can jump now," Sally thought. "Even if I do make mistakes and get mixed up, it doesn't matter—I can jump." She rode back to Thalia grinning broadly, because she knew now, and nothing could change it.

Normally Thalia would have gathered up Tarquin's reins and sent him galloping wildly over the jumps, but today she didn't. She circled Tarquin at a trot, then at a slow canter. She halted him, then rode forward and halted again. Then she trotted him in a circle, only letting him canter as they rode at the first jump.

After the barrels, when normally Tarquin would have been charging madly on, more or less out of control, Thalia turned him away from the jumps. Trotting in circles, she settled him before they cleared the last two jumps.

"I've changed," Thalia announced, walking

on a loose rein over to Sally. "Not for cross-country. If in doubt, kick them on. But, I suppose, for show jumping he is a bit crazy."

"They've all been telling you that for months!"

"It was Charlotte who did it. I could hardly stop Tarquin after the show jumping against the Haxton team. We almost galloped straight into Charlotte and her mother. She says in her big, loud, pimply voice, 'Don't mind us. Out of control as usual?' Then she laughed. You know the way she does. So I thought . . . perhaps I should. . . . So that's why."

By lunchtime the vet still hadn't been to see Meg. When Sally had finished her lunch, she sat down beside Meg where she lay on her rug in front of the fire.

"You're a good, dear Meg," she said. "When Dr. Cheever comes this afternoon, he'll say you're a lot better. I know he will."

Meg lifted her head and thumped the rug with her tail, but she didn't really want to be bothered with anyone. Not even Sally. She let her head drop back onto the rug and in seconds she was asleep again, the sound of her noisy breathing filling the kitchen.

"Try not to upset yourself too much," said her mother. "She's still eating well and poddling about the garden when she feels like it. Why don't you take Misty for a walk? She hasn't had a decent walk for days."

Sally took Misty down to the shore and threw sticks for her. Barking at her absolute loudest, Misty raced after the sticks, leaping and jumping in furious tornadoes of white and gray hair.

But Sally couldn't stop wondering if the vet had already come and gone or if he might be at Kestrel Manor at that very moment. She whistled for Misty and began to walk home. As she went along, her eyes searched Kestrel Manor's grounds for any sign of the white hound, but there was only the autumn tangle of leaves, dying grasses, and dense bushes. No white shape was waiting in the undergrowth or racing over the muddied lawns. And when she got home the vet still hadn't been there.

Thalia and Sally rode in the afternoon and then cleaned tack and groomed.

"Perhaps it's a different dog that frightened

the children," suggested Thalia as she worked on Tarquin's mane. "Maybe the men took their dog away with them."

"No," Sally shouted in reply as she scrubbed at Willow's muddied fetlocks. "They were gone the last time I saw the dog. They left her behind. Who's feeding her now? Who's looking after her?"

Thalia had no answers, and Sally did not know what else she could do to find the dog. She had left her unicorn at her window so it would be there if the hound came to Kestrel Manor. Sally knew that everyone else would think it was silly nonsense, but it hadn't stopped her from standing the unicorn securely on the windowsill and leaving it there all the time.

Mr. Lorimer had come back from his library, Ben had come home from school, and there was still no vet. They all ate their supper with ears alert for the vet's car, but it wasn't until Ben and Sally had finished washing up and Jamie had spread out his train set for a last ten minutes before he went to bed that there was a knock on the door.

Ben hurried to open it, with Sally close behind him.

A small, dark-haired man in a tweed cap, waxed jacket, and Wellington boots stood there.

"Good evening," he said, showing false teeth as he smiled at them. "Is your dad in?"

"Evening," said Mr. Lorimer, coming to the door. "Can I help you?"

"I'm Hugh Brown, dog warden." The man took a plastic card from his pocket and flickered it in front of Mr. Lorimer. "Could I have a few words with you about a white greyhound? I believe it's been seen around here."

"Come in," said Mr. Lorimer. Hugh Brown came into the kitchen and perched on the edge of a chair. Sally stared at him, hating everything about him. How dare he come into her house, hunting down the white hound? Sally knew what the dogcatcher would do if he caught the hound. He would kill her.

"It seems to have been abandoned. Nasty-natured beast. Went after a little boy in Fintry."

"You mean it bit him?" asked Mr. Lorimer.

"Not exactly. A near thing. Lucky his mom was there to chase the dog off or we'd have had a TV interview on our hands. Once you get a dog who's a loner like this one, no telling what it'll do next."

Sally stood with her back to the door, scowling at the dogcatcher.

"The white hound's not like that," she said. "She's a beautiful dog. She would never hurt anyone!"

"Ah," said the dogcatcher. "So you've seen her? Prowling around your grounds?"

Sally blushed scarlet.

"No!" she said. "Of course I haven't seen her. She's never been here."

"Didn't you see a white dog from your bedroom window?" asked her mother. "You told us about it. Perhaps it was the same dog?"

"That wasn't the white hound . . ." Sally began, and then stopped, realizing that the more she said the worse she made things.

"I must warn you not to go near the dog. She could be dangerous. If you see her, phone the police and they'll contact me."

Mr. Lorimer said they all understood. They'd let the warden know if there was any sign of the dog.

"Never," thought Sally. "I'd never call the police." Sally knew that some dogs could be dangerous. She had read about it in the papers.

Seen the horrible photographs of children with torn faces. She was certain that the hound wasn't like that. Not vicious. Abandoned and afraid, but not vicious. Sally could not believe that such a calm, gentle dog could be dangerous.

"Would it be all right if I have a look around your grounds tomorrow?" asked the dog-catcher. Mr. Lorimer said it would.

The vet arrived minutes after the dogcatcher left. He was in a hurry, going straight to Meg, uncoiling his stethoscope as he went. But when he listened to Meg's heart he slowed down, listening carefully, giving her his full attention.

All the Lorimers waited tensely until he stood up. "Is she eating?" he asked. "No trouble with her bowels?"

"She's fine," said Mrs. Lorimer. "Drinking more than she used to and doesn't want to move much. Out for a few minutes and then back in to lie down again."

"Right," said the vet. "I don't like the sound of her heart tonight. Thought it might have steadied a bit by now. There is one thing we could try. Bit of a gamble. Might work, might not. It boosts the whole system. It depends how strong the dog is, whether she can pull through on it or not. If it works for her, things would be looking good."

"Sounds rather desperate," said Mr. Lorimer.

"It is," said the vet. "But I think in Meg's case we are going to have to consider it. I'll come back tomorrow, have another listen, and we can make the decision then."

The vet gave Meg an injection, then crouched down and spoke to her. He ran his hand gently over her head, telling her she was a brave old lady, while Meg regarded him calmly from deep-brown eyes.

Sally took Meg out before she went to bed. She helped her down the step and waited while Meg sniffed about in the grass.

On their way back into the house Meg sat down on the doorstep. Sally stopped beside her. She couldn't bear to think that Meg was going to die.

Sally knelt beside Meg and took her head in both her hands.

"Listen," she said, speaking directly to Meg. "You are not going to die. You are going to get better."

Chapter Seven

"Why couldn't you all have ridden like that last week?" demanded Mrs. Blair, looking around at her team as they stood holding their horses and listening to her. They had just spent the afternoon being instructed by Martine as they repeated the cross-country and show-jumping courses that they had ridden last weekend against the Haxton team.

"I forgot my gloves," said Sally. "Then everything else went wrong."

"They were all such snobs," said Thalia. "All looking down their noses at us."

"You knew they were the best," Verity said accusingly. "You knew how good they were before you invited them."

Mrs. Blair laughed. "Perhaps I did," she admitted. "It let you know what you'll be up against. They will be there on Saturday, so that gives you the chance to get even."

"We will," said Thalia.

Martine had been very pleased by the way

Tarquin had calmed down when he was show
jumping. Thalia had her praise stored in her
mind. She would listen to it properly when she
was alone.

"Now," said Mrs. Blair, checking the lists in
her hand. "I've spoken to your parents. They
are all coming. We will need first-class support.
On Saturday morning you will all be here at
eight o'clock. Martine is bringing Sally and
Thalia and their horses. Verity is here, and
Simon, your father is bringing you and Zodiac
in your trailer. You can stable her here. You're
sure that Zodiac will be fully shod for the
Event?"

"She will," said Simon, looking down at the
ground.

Simon had arrived riding Clover, telling
them that Zodiac had cast a shoe and couldn't
be ridden until the blacksmith came. Simon
had not jumped the cross-country obstacles,
saying that Clover was not fit.

Sally had been delighted to see Clover
again. She was looking sleek and contented and
years younger than she had as a riding-school
pony at Miss Meek's. Simon, too, looked as if he

was enjoying riding her. Sally remembered how white and strained Simon had looked when he led Zodiac away from the cross-country. Although he had ridden in the show-jumping phase, he had had three refusals at the first jump and had not remounted in the cross-country.

"Stop it!" Sally told herself. "You're getting as bad as Charlotte." She turned her attention back to Mrs. Blair just in time to hear Mrs. Blair tell her to pin a clean pair of gloves to her jacket sleeve.

"If you need help, let me know," said Martine as they unloaded Willow and Tarquin in Kestrel Manor's yard. "I'll call on Friday evening to cheer you on. Keep up the good work with Tarquin. I'm expecting an A-plus dressage test. And Sally, remember to look up; look over the jump, not at it."

Now that she was home, Sally only wanted to find out how Meg was. She took Willow's tack off and put the water bucket into her stall. Tossing in an armful of hay, she told Thalia that she would be back in a minute.

Through the lighted kitchen window Sally

saw Meg lying flat on the hearth rug, her breathing lifting her whole body. Misty and Mrs. Lorimer were busy at the stove.

"How is she?" Sally cried, dashing into the kitchen.

Her mother turned around quickly, her finger to her lips. Misty bounded to meet her, but Meg didn't move.

"Shhh! Don't disturb her. We had to phone the vet. She had another turn."

"What did he say?" demanded Sally urgently, speaking from a far, cold place, her voice frozen to a whisper.

"He's changed her pills to the ones he told us about. There is a risk, but at least they'll give her a chance."

Sally's eyes filled with tears. She wanted her mother to comfort her. But Mrs. Lorimer, searching in her apron for her handkerchief, was crying herself.

"He says we shouldn't give up hope. There's a good chance that she'll pull through."

Sally stood looking down at Meg, listening to the gasp and drag of her breathing.

"Don't disturb her," Mrs. Lorimer warned

again. "The more she sleeps, the better. We've got to keep her as quiet as possible. Only fish or chicken and well-boiled brown rice. It will be a week before we'll know whether she can cope with the pills."

Sally turned away and went back to Willow. She threw her arms around her horse's neck and buried her face in Willow's mane.

"Is it Meg?" asked Thalia, standing hesitantly in the doorway.

"She's had another heart attack," mumbled Sally.

"You mean she's not dead?" cried Thalia. "Well, that's good. If she's not dead, then there's lots that we can do for her."

Sally explained what the vet had said.

"That means we have the whole of medical science working for us! What we've got to do is help Meg. We've got to think of her as she will be—completely better. Running and barking and chasing Misty. That's what Narg always does. I'll tell her to think about Meg. Don't think for a second that she might not get better. Imagine her well and happy again."

Sally lifted her head, scrubbed at her eyes

with a tissue, and pushed her hair back behind her ears.

"Imagine her well all the time," insisted Thalia.

Sally pictured Meg coming into the stall, sitting down to wait for her as she had done so many times, her bright eyes gleaming through her shaggy hair and her black nose glistening. As Sally walked back home, leaving Willow with a deep straw bed and a full hay net, she imagined Meg running in front of her, barking impatiently.

"Did anyone tell Sally about the meat?" Ben asked as they were finishing their meal.

"What meat?" Sally asked.

"Obviously not," said her father. "The dog-catcher came back while you were at Mrs. Blair's. He had a look around and thinks the white dog may have been sleeping in the summerhouse. There's an old rug there and it's covered with white hairs. He's left some drugged meat near the rug, hoping the dog will come back tonight, eat it, and fall asleep. If it does, it should still be there in the morning when he comes to check up. No one is to go near the summerhouse."

Strong feelings flooded over Sally—guilt that the white hound had been living at Kestrel Manor and she hadn't known, fury that the dog-catcher had been to Kestrel Manor, mixed with rage that he had dared to leave drugged meat in their summerhouse.

"It might be drugged meat for a hound," exclaimed Sally, her voice loud and shouting, not at all a supper-table voice. "But what about a cat or a fox? It would be poison for them."

"He promised us that it was not poisoned. It will only make any animal unconscious."

"If the dog is as dangerous as he says it is, we must help him to catch it," said Mrs. Lorimer. "You can't have dogs going around attacking children. Be sensible, Sally."

Sally gazed despairingly at her parents. She had tried to explain to them that she had seen the hound, that it was quiet and gentle and beautiful, that she understood that stray dogs could be dangerous but that the hound was not. She knew that once her parents saw the hound, they would understand. But she could not make them listen to her.

Mrs. Lorimer gave Meg her pills. She took

them without any fuss, then pulled herself
stiffly to her feet and walked the few steps to
her bowl. She stood for a minute until she got
her balance, then lowered her head to lap the
water. When she finished, she turned without
looking at any of them and slowly reached her
rug again. Her legs gave way and she collapsed.
In seconds she was asleep again.

Sally caught the quick look that passed
between her mother and father. Instantly she
knew what they were thinking—that it would
be the kindest thing to have Meg put down.

"We all have to think of her as being well
again. Thalia says that's what her narg does.
You must not feel sorry for her but keep imagining she's better."

To Sally's surprise no one argued with her.
Even Jamie scrunched up his face and said he
could see Meg eating candies he had given her.

Sally waited until all her family had settled
to their evening occupations—Ben to his books,
her father to doze in front of the television, and
her mother to read Jamie his bedtime story.

Sally left the living room quietly. In the
kitchen she pulled on her jacket and found a

plastic bag in the drawer. Picking up the flashlight from its place on the counter, she silently opened the door. She crept through, closed it, and listened. She had escaped. Misty had not heard her.

Sally followed the bobbing yellow light of her flashlight across the grass, through the autumn tangle of bushes and shrubs. At last she saw the summerhouse and, beyond it, the moonlit glitter of the black, quicksilver sea.

Sally stood still, swinging her flashlight in wide swaths of yellow light. Nothing moved. There was no sign of the white hound. Sally shivered, suddenly wishing that she had brought Misty with her or gone for Thalia. But she knew that she would never find the white hound if there was someone else with her. She had to wait in the summerhouse by herself.

The dogcatcher had put the meat on the floor, close to the old blanket that had been left lying there. Sally put her hand into the plastic bag, picked up the meat, then pulled the bag over it. She had picked it up without touching it. No matter what the dogcatcher had said, Sally was sure it was poisoned.

She sat down on the window seat and folded her arms. Then, staring out into the dark, moon-gleaming gardens, she waited for the hound to come.

First Sally concentrated on seeing Meg well again. Then she rode Willow through the dressage test. Her head nodded and her eyes closed.

Willow and Tarquin had wings. Thalia and Sally raced them over a sea the color of amethyst and over banks of white cloud. As they rode, someone was watching them.

Sally's eyelids twitched. She woke from her dream, realizing that she had been asleep. Yet part of the dream was real. There was someone watching her. Cautiously she opened her eyes. Framed in the doorway of the summerhouse stood the white hound.

For a second Sally felt her skin creep and her spine tighten. The hound seemed to have come from a dark world of enchanted fairy tales. Then Sally moved slightly and the dog walked toward her, hardly disturbing the darkness. Her long, fine legs, arched neck, and high, lean body moved in silence.

She came right up to Sally, placed a knuckled paw on her knee, and laid her almost weightless head in Sally's lap. She stood perfectly still, gazing up at Sally with loyalty and love.

Chapter Eight

Sally held her breath, terrified that if she moved she would frighten the hound. But the dog did not seem to be afraid at all. She gazed up at Sally with her strange, blue-white eyes. Only the tip of her sickle tail moved from side to side.

Gradually Sally ran her hand down the hound's neck and along the knotted ridge of her spine. Sally felt the dog's ribs stretching through her harsh skin and realized how thin she was, even for a greyhound.

"Poor dog," she whispered. "Did those men leave you behind? But you're my dog now. I'm going to keep you. I don't care what anyone says—you're going to stay with us. You need a name. That will make you belong to us."

Sally thought of dog names. It had to be the right name. She waited for it to come into her mind.

"Fenella," she said at last. "I shall call you Fen."

The hound, who had been listening intently, pawed at Sally's knee and pushed at her elbow with her long muzzle.

"That's it: Fen.

"Now, stay with me," Sally said, standing up slowly, terrified that the hound would race away and vanish into the dark. There was no handful of Beardie hair to grasp. Nothing to hold on to.

Step by step, Sally set off along the path to Kestrel Manor. Fen moved gracefully at her side, showing no signs of wanting to leave her.

As the lighted windows of Kestrel Manor came into sight, Sally hesitated, wondering what her family would say. Would her mother want another dog, especially when the dog-catcher thought she might be dangerous? Would she be all right with Meg?—for nothing must be allowed to disturb Meg.

Fen looked up questioningly, a front paw lifted.

"Of course they'll want you," Sally told her. "Of course they will." She marched on into the house.

"Where on earth did you find her?" demanded her father.

"She is some size," said her mother.

"But beautiful!" exclaimed Ben, coming to stroke her.

Fen paid no attention to anyone, not even to Misty, who was bounding and barking just out of Fen's reach. The hound stood by Sally's side, gazing mildly around the kitchen. She saw Meg lying in front of the fire and walked across to her. Fen looked down and Meg startled awake. She lifted her head up, and Fen stretched her neck out so that their noses almost touched. There was a moment of silence, then Meg gave a gusty sigh and lay down again, putting her head carefully on the rug, not letting it fall back because she was too exhausted to do anything else.

And in that moment Sally was filled with a certainty that Meg would get better.

"She's going to be all right . . ." Sally began, turning to her family, but no one was paying any attention to her.

Mrs. Lorimer was warning Jamie not to go too close to the hound, her father was looking up the dogcatcher's telephone number, and Ben was opening a can of dog food.

"She's ours," Sally said to her father. "She belongs to me. I've named her Fen, so we must keep her. Please don't phone the dogcatcher. He doesn't need to know I found her. We can keep her and just not tell him."

"No, Sally. Of course we must let him know," said Mr. Lorimer. He phoned the dog-catcher and left a message.

"But you won't let him take her away?"

"We'll see what he has to say," said Mr. Lorimer. "If he still thinks she is dangerous, she will have to go."

"Honestly, she doesn't look dangerous to me," said Ben, stroking Fen. "She's a super dog. I vote we keep her."

Fen had eaten the food that Ben had given to her, had a drink, and was lying by the table watching them all through gentle eyes. Her long ivory legs were sprawled out on the carpet, her knuckled paws folded over. She completely ignored Misty, who was sniffing her.

"She's certainly made herself at home," said Mr. Lorimer.

"That's because she is at home," said Sally. "Kestrel Manor is her home."

"She does seem like a nice dog," admitted Mr. Lorimer. "Perhaps she wouldn't be any trouble."

" 'Nice'!" thought Sally. How could her father possibly see Fen as "nice"? She was a hound from King Arthur's court who had ridden out with the knights, or a hound from an Egyptian temple led out by the priests in procession behind the god king.

"We *must* keep her," she said.

"Don't upset yourself tonight," said her mother. "I don't think there's any chance of the dogcatcher coming out now. Much too late."

Sally supposed not. Reluctantly she got out her homework.

The knock on the door made them all jump. No one had heard a car.

"Hide her!" cried Sally desperately, sure it must be the dogcatcher.

"Don't be silly," warned her mother as Mr. Lorimer brought the dogcatcher into the kitchen.

"That's her all right," said the dogcatcher, seeing the hound at once in spite of Sally's efforts to stand in front of Fen. "Any trouble? I'll take her away with me."

"No!" cried Sally desperately. "She is my dog. You can't have her!"

The dogcatcher took a leather collar from his pocket and buckled it around the white hound's neck.

"Seems quiet enough now," he said.

"Of course she is," cried Sally, and she flung her arms around Fen, trying to pull her away from the dogcatcher.

"You know what Sally will be like if we don't keep her," said Ben. "Tears and torment for weeks."

The dogcatcher let the hound go, and Sally pulled her close to her side.

Mrs. Lorimer looked at Mr. Lorimer, lifting her eyebrows. Mr. Lorimer looked at the dogcatcher, who pushed his hand through his hair.

"There seems to have been only one incident involving a child," he admitted. "I tracked down the parents this afternoon. Their boy had a bag of chips, and I reckon he was teasing the dog. Offering her a chip and then snatching it away from her. All she did was bark at him. Then the boy blew up the chip bag and burst it in her face. She bolted, knocked the boy over, and all the rumors grew from that."

"Would it be all right if we kept her?" said Mrs. Lorimer. "I can't bear to think of her being put down."

"Oh, thank you! Thank you!" cried Sally in delight.

"Not easy for me, either," said the dog-catcher. He paused. "You seem like a family that's used to dogs. I'll chance it. Leave her with you for a week. Any sign of bad temper, you must let me know at once and I'll be out for her."

"Oh, but you won't need to come back," Sally assured him. "We'll look after her forever."

"I'll be around next Saturday."

"That's the one-day event," said Mrs. Lorimer. "We may all be out."

"Evening, then," said the dogcatcher. He took forms out of his inside pocket for Mr. Lorimer to sign.

Sally went quietly to bed, not saying good night to anyone. Fen walked at her heels. If Mrs. Lorimer saw, she said nothing.

Fen curled up on the mat by Sally's bed, her long muzzle tucked into the crook of her leg. Sitting up in bed, Sally looked from the tiny shape of the unicorn silhouetted against the sky to the ivory hound, sleeping as peacefully as if she had lived with the Lorimers all her life.

In a week, in only seven short days, the dog-catcher would be back, they would know if the pills were working for Meg, and it would be the one-day event. Be now. Be over. A day to be remembered. Sally wrapped her arms around herself, shivering with a mixture of delight and fear. Her head touched her pillow and she slept.

Thalia was miffed that Sally had not called her when she found Fen.

"You might have needed me. I could have let out his tires to keep him from taking Fen away!"

The vet came to see Meg on Wednesday.

"He's pleased with her," Mrs. Lorimer told Sally when she came in from school.

As if she knew what they were saying, Meg sat up, wagging her tail, and crossed the room to Sally.

"You are a bit better," cried Sally, dropping

on her knees to stroke Meg. She was afraid to say more, just in case. "Dear dog, dear, dear Meg."

Misty came leaping and bounding about them, but Fen waited quietly by Meg's side, making sure that Misty didn't knock the older Beardie over.

"The vet can't be certain until the end of the week, but the pills do seem to be agreeing with her," Mrs. Lorimer said as Meg snuffled her face into Sally's jacket pocket, smelling a cookie that Sally had forgotten about. When she couldn't reach it, Meg sat down and barked her command that Sally should give her the cookie immediately. Gobbling it up, Meg seemed almost her old self again.

The Friday before the one-day event was the longest, slowest school day that Sally and Thalia had ever known, but when they got home to Kestrel Manor, the evening vanished in the stamp of a horse's hoof.

Right after school they rode their horses down to the shore and schooled them, each thinking the same thing—that the next time they rode, it would be in the one-day event.

Thalia was sleeping at Kestrel Manor, so when they had finished eating Mrs. Lorimer's homemade pie, they went out to the stables and groomed until their arms ached and their horses shone.

"Now for the tack," said Thalia, refusing to give in to Sally's suggestion that they have a drink of juice before they started.

Mrs. Lorimer made them go to bed early.

"If you have to be up at five, you must get some sleep," she insisted. "Off you go."

They sat up in bed, taking turns going over the dressage test, pushing one of Sally's china horses around the bedspread. Their riding clothes, washed and ironed by Mrs. Lorimer and Narg, hung outside the closet door. A pair of yellow string gloves was pinned to the sleeve of Sally's jacket, and Thalia's new hat hung from its own hook on the back of the door. Mr. Lorimer had polished their boots, and their shine would have passed any sergeant major's examination.

"Tomorrow," said Sally. "Everything is waiting for tomorrow. Willow and Tarquin and all the other horses and their riders."

"Clean tack and clean clothes," said Thalia. "Especially my hat."

"Gas in the horse trailer. Cross-country obstacles."

"Martine and Mrs. Blair wanting us to do well," said Thalia. "The Tarent team sure they are going to win."

"And me," said Sally. "Me who could hardly ride at all a few months ago." And the thought of tomorrow swept over Sally like the sea.

Chapter Nine

M artine drove the horse trailer into the parking area of Leighton Hall. Horses were being unloaded, bandages taken off and girths checked while children and parents shouted at each other in loud, excited voices. Peering from the cab window, Sally and Thalia could see nothing but bustle and action. When they jumped out, they could feel the excitement in the air.

"It's all real," Sally thought. "I am here to ride in a one-day event. It's not a horse book I'm reading. It is really going to happen!"

Verity and Simon, who had come in their parents' cars, came running across to them.

"Dad's been yelling his head off," said Simon. "Thinks I'm not going to have enough time to ride Zodiac in."

"Well, he can stop worrying now. We have arrived," said Martine. She took them across to the edge of the parking area. "This will give you an idea of where you are."

From where they stood on a rise in the ground, they could see the one-day event spread out before them. There was the practice area, a rough field where several horses were being ridden in; the newly mown dressage area, with brightly painted white letters set correctly around its edges; the roped-in show-jumping ring; and, curving out of sight between a broad river and a clump of lime trees, the beginning of the cross-country course. They could see the first two jumps—rustic poles and a brush jump. Red flag markers on the right of the obstacles and white flag markers on the left hung limply in the moist air.

"Remember," said Martine. "You must ride between the flags or you'll be eliminated."

"But we will be walking around the cross-country, won't we?" asked Simon.

Sally, hearing the strain in his voice, looked around at Simon. His face was drawn and tense, his lips closed into a tight line and his eyebrows gathered in. He looked every bit as nervous as he had before the Tarent show.

"With me to guide you every hoofprint of the way," Martine assured him.

Mrs. Blair came bustling toward them.

"Time you were all mounted," she said, shooing them back to the horse trailer. "Now, I only expect one thing—that you all do your best. Sally, you've got your gloves? Thalia, we do not want any rodeo displays."

Martine slipped down to the back of the horse trailer. Speaking calmly to the horses, she began to untie their halter ropes and hand them to their riders.

Verity led Buster out. Zodiac plunged down the ramp, almost dragging Simon off his feet. Sally took Willow, and Thalia shouted at Tarquin, yanked at his halter rope, and managed to keep him to a walk as he clattered out of the trailer.

Glancing back into the gaping black cave of the horse trailer, Sally thought she saw something moving. From a pile of rugs and blankets at the very back of the trailer, a long white hound's face looked out at them. Two slender, bony legs pushed through beneath the face, and Fen flowed down from between the blankets.

"Yikes!" cried Martine, seeing Fen at the same time as Sally. "How on earth did she get here?"

Knowing she had done wrong, Fen slunk out of the trailer and crouched down close to Sally.

Mrs. Blair was not amused.

"Put her in the cab and leave her there until your parents arrive," she told Sally. "They can do what they like with her. You are about to ride a dressage test."

Shut in the cab of the horse trailer, Fen scrabbled wildly, tearing at the window, trying to open it.

"Leave her alone," Mrs. Blair warned Sally, and began to check over her team's riding clothes and their horses' tack.

All the time Mrs. Blair was speaking, Fen kept up her furious attempts to escape.

"This is no good," cried Martine in exasperation. "We can't let her go on creating that racket." She wrenched open the cab door, letting Fen leap to the ground and race to Sally's side.

"When are your parents coming?" demanded Mrs. Blair.

"Soon," said Sally, feeling it was all her fault but not quite knowing why. "They were planning to leave not long after we did."

The others rode down to the schooling area while Mrs. Blair found a rope lead in the trunk of her car and looped it around Fen's neck. But when Sally rode away, Fen pulled free from Mrs. Blair and charged after Sally.

"Oh, honestly!" shouted Mrs. Blair. "Dratted dog! Well, I must see about your entries. You'll need to dismount and come with me to the secretary's trailer."

Holding Fen by the rope and Willow by her reins, Sally stood outside the trailer, watching the others riding in their horses and wishing desperately that her parents would arrive.

Mrs. Blair came out of the trailer with their show numbers and called her team together.

"As you know, our team's drawn second to last in the running order. Thalia, you're thirteen, Sally, fourteen, Simon, fifteen, and Verity, sixteen. That's your order in all phases.

"Lucky you're almost last," Mrs. Blair said to Sally. "It should give your parents time to get here and take over the hound."

"And the rest of you," said Martine, "go on and wake your horses up. Some hard schooling. Get them to pay attention to you."

"Be best if you wait by the horse trailer," Mrs. Blair said to Sally. "You'll see your family driving in. Now, don't worry. I'll come back and we'll straighten things out in plenty of time." Mrs. Blair hurried off, shouting to Verity to kick Buster on.

Sally found a place where she could see the dressage arena and watch for the Lorimers' car. People passing stared curiously at her. Several adults stopped to ask if they could help, and Sally told them that she was all right, just waiting.

One by one she saw horses leave the practice area, wait for their turn to ride into the arena, and, like clockwork toys, each follow exactly the same pattern before they rode out again.

"I should be there," Sally thought despairingly. "We're going to miss our turn. It's not fair. Not fair. Oh, Fen, it's your fault. You should have stayed at home." But a bit of Sally couldn't help being pleased that Fen had stowed away to be with her.

"Darling," cried Mrs. Lorimer, running toward her daughter. "How on earth did Fen get here? And why are you by yourself? Shouldn't you be riding?"

"She came with us in the trailer. I didn't know she was there, and she won't behave herself without me. The dressage started ages ago, and I should be riding Willow in before it's my turn."

"Right," said Mrs. Lorimer, asking no more questions. "Let me have Fen."

She took the rope from Sally, and Fen greeted Mr. Lorimer, Ben, and Jamie with her sharp, tight bark.

Hardly pausing to thank her family, Sally trotted Willow over to the field and started to ride her in.

Willow had been bored being dragged about by her reins, not understanding what was happening. Now she pricked her ears and walked out with a long stride. She trotted and cantered freely when Sally asked her to, changing her paces smoothly. As she rode, Sally forgot about the muddle of the morning and the trouble with Fen. She was thinking only of Willow, riding as if she really was part of her horse.

Waiting by the dressage arena, Sally watched Thalia ride her test, holding her breath when Tarquin's canter became a pounding gallop.

The judge tooted her horn.

"They're ready for you," said Martine.

Sally took a deep breath and rode into the arena. At the center she halted Willow, who stood four-square without a movement while Sally dropped her right hand, correct in its yellow glove, to her side, and saluted the judge with a nod of her head.

She had ridden the complete dressage test only once before, but now all Sally's hours of schooling stood her in good stead. The different movements fell into place as easily as the correct pieces of a jigsaw puzzle. Willow's trot took her into the corners of the arena. She turned smartly, changing pace accurately at the correct letter. All Willow's movements were calm and smooth as Sally rode her through the test. In what seemed to Sally no time at all, she had completed the last movement, saluted the judge, and was riding out of the arena at a free walk on a loose rein.

"That," said Martine, "was really something!"

"It just happened," Sally said. "It was all Willow." She hid her face in Willow's mane to hide her embarrassment at having done so well.

When the results of the dressage were posted in the window of the trailer, Sally had the lowest number of penalty points, which meant she was first in the dressage phase. Verity was eighth, Thalia thirteenth, and Simon fifteenth.

"Fantastic!" cried Thalia. "Absolutely amazing!"

"It's not over yet," cautioned Mrs. Blair.

"Of course," agreed Thalia, "it is the cross-country that really matters."

During the lunch break they walked the cross-country. After the first two jumps there were three jumps among the trees, then a drop jump with a pole in front of it, and a water jump over the river. After that they were to gallop on over a string of jumps stretching out over the open country.

Sally listened intently to Martine's instructions. She studied the obstacles, thinking how she would tackle them. She had totally forgotten to be afraid.

"It's absolutely super," enthused Thalia. "Tarquin will fly around it."

"One thing about Buster," said Verity, "is that he knows how to look after himself. We won't be first, but we'll be safest."

Only Simon knew that the drop jump out of the wood was exactly the same as the jump where he had had his accident.

"It's about an hour before the cross-country starts," said Martine. "Get yourselves organized. Change into your sweaters. You all know your starting time? We'll be watching out for you. Good luck to you all."

Sally was riding Willow in when she suddenly saw Fen racing toward her.

"Where have you been?" Sally cried, seeing that Fen's legs, shoulder, and head were covered with black, gleaming mud. "What's happened to you?"

Fen raced straight up to Sally and gripped the heel of Sally's boot in her jaws. Then she let go of it, ran off for a few strides, and stood barking at Sally, obviously wanting Sally to follow her.

"What do you want?" Sally demanded, then stopped in horror. A glint of sun on Fen's muddied head and shoulder showed something that Sally had not noticed before.

Although Fen was not injured, the side of her head and down her neck to her shoulder were bright with blood.

Chapter Ten

S ally froze. For a moment of blind panic she could only hear the dogcatcher's warnings, could only think that Fen had attacked a child.

Fen came running back and gripped Sally's boot again. Tugging wildly, she tried to make Sally pay attention to her.

For a second Sally looked around for help; then she realized that, whatever had happened, she had to find out the truth for herself.

Fen ran in front of Sally, who urged Willow into a gallop to keep up with her. They raced toward the river, in the opposite direction from the cross-country. Fen leaped down from the field to a broad strand of riverbank. Rocks set in the smooth-flowing river churned it into torrents of foam.

Lying on the bank, just clear of the rocks and the river, was a little boy who looked about three years old. His face was scraped and bleeding and his fair hair sticky with blood from a

gash on his head. For a split second Sally
thought that Fen had attacked him, and then
she saw the trail on the bank where he had
been pulled from the water. She watched Fen
grab his coat and try to pull him farther away
from the river.

Sally leaped down from Willow, remembering that you should never try to move anyone
who has had an accident. She loosened the
child's clothing with fumbling hands. Although
he was unconscious, he was breathing easily.

Telling Fen to stay, Sally jumped back onto
Willow and galloped for help. There was an
ambulance at the start of the cross-country.
Sally charged through horses and riders, past
spectators and stewards. Reaching the ambulance, she shouted for help.

By the time the ambulance reached the
little boy, several people who had seen Sally
and Fen galloping to the river had come over
to find out what was happening. Ben was
there, with Fen securely held by her rope, as
was the child's mother, who had been searching everywhere for her son. The ambulance
men lifted the child onto a stretcher, and with

his mother beside him, they drove away.

"We'd gone back to the car for a drink of juice," explained Ben. "Fen had settled down on the backseat. She didn't seem to want to come with us when we were ready to go back to the cross-country, so we left her. The window was a bit open. She must have squeezed through and gone to the river for a drink."

Sally wanted to say it was a good thing, for if Fen hadn't found the child, he might have drowned. She wanted to tell Ben how clever Fen was, dragging the child to safety, but her teeth were chattering so much she couldn't speak. She leaned against Willow, shivering uncontrollably.

"Have you ridden in the cross-country?" Ben asked.

Sally shook her head. She could hardly bring her mind back to thoughts of the cross-country, she was so relieved that Fen had not attacked the little boy.

Thalia came charging up on Tarquin.

"They sent me to find you," she shouted. "Hurry up. It'll be our turn in about twenty minutes. What's wrong? Are you ill?"

Ben explained.

"But she's got to ride!" exclaimed Thalia. "It's for the team. She must."

Somehow Sally forced her rubbery legs to climb back onto Willow. Once she was riding again, she felt better. The cross-country mattered; the team was real again.

Sally hardly had time to ride Willow in before it was time for the Tarent team to ride. Thalia was to go first, Sally second, Simon third, and Verity last. There were two minutes between each start.

Waiting, Sally saw Thalia go galloping out, clear the rustic poles, gallop on and over the stone wall, swing right and on out of sight into the shelter of the trees.

Sally gathered Willow together, niggling with her heels on her sides and her fingers on the reins.

"We'll do it. We'll do it easily," she told Willow. As she galloped free from the start, she was filled with energy and excitement. The cross-country was a challenge, a delight.

With pounding hooves and pricked ears, Willow carried Sally over the first two jumps.

She swung around into the trail between the trees and bounced over a white-painted gate. There was one more jump over a fallen tree trunk before the trail sloped downhill.

Sally heard Martine's voice warning them to steady their horses before they rode downhill. Sitting down in the saddle, she tightened her hands on Willow's reins and felt her horse's canter change to a trot.

A row of painted barrels stretched across the steep trail. Willow goggled suspiciously at them, but Sally drove her on and Willow leaped suddenly and sharply into the air to clear them. She touched down, and in another few strides they were over the pole in front of the drop and out of the wood.

The water jump was next. Willow took off well before they reached the bank of the river, which was churned into deep mud by galloping hooves. Willow leaped in a low arc over the poles set in the middle of the river, to land far out on the other side. The open course spread out before them.

Remembering time faults, Sally pushed her horse on, and Willow responded willingly.

Never before had Sally ridden like this; never before had she known such freedom.

From the corner of her eye she glimpsed red flags on the right side, saw stewards with clipboards, but they were no part of Sally's flying ecstasy. She rode over the short turf, under the high, blue autumn sky as if there were only herself and her horse jumping and galloping in a newly created world.

They reached the farthest point of the course and circled around toward the finish. They rode over wattle fencing, jumped in and out of a sheep pen, over a brush fence and a spread of poles over a ditch. The last fence was a painted wishing well, which Willow cleared with a soaring leap and then galloped on through the finish.

"You made it!" yelled Thalia. "How did it go?"

Sally flung her reins loose and threw her arms around Willow's neck. It was too soon to come back to the world of Thalia and winning. Too soon. She wanted to stay in the bewitched magic world of galloping and jumping.

"Did she have any refusals? Did she stop?"

Sally shook her head and slid down from

Willow, patting her and thanking her.

"Well? What happened? Tell me!"

Thalia was not to be denied.

"I don't know," said Sally. "I think we were clear. But it was super. Absolutely super."

Words weren't enough. She couldn't begin to tell Thalia.

"So was I. Clear. So was I," rejoiced Thalia.

Mrs. Blair came hurrying across with blankets, asking questions, telling them to loosen their horses' girths, ease off their saddles, and walk their horses around to cool them off before taking them back to the trailer.

Simon and Zodiac were covered in mud when they rode through the finish, and had obviously had a fall.

"Are you all right?" demanded Mrs. Blair.

"It was the drop out of the wood," Simon told them. "She took a huge leap and I came off over her head. But I'm fine. Honestly. Zodiac slipped, but she didn't come down. All I was thinking about was holding on to my reins so we could jump the rest of the course. I wasn't a bit scared. Just felt like I used to before Merlin and I crashed."

"Well done," said Mrs. Blair.

"Fantastic," said Thalia.

Simon slid to the ground.

"She's going to be a real cross-country horse," he said, patting Zodiac's neck. "Even better than Merlin. The best I've ever ridden." And he was grinning from ear to ear.

Verity finished at a trot.

"Four refusals, and I think we exceeded the time limit."

She was right. When the results were posted, she had been eliminated. Simon's collection of penalty points put him at the bottom, and Thalia, to her loud disgust, had been eliminated for taking the wrong course at the water jump. She had forgotten about the flags and jumped with the red flag on her left. Two eliminations meant that the team was out of the event.

But Sally was clear—no penalty points, no time points. A boy from the Haxton team was in second place, close behind Sally. If he jumped clear in the show jumping and Sally had a knockdown, he would be first.

Both Thalia and Verity were allowed to take part in the show jumping but not to compete.

Waiting for her turn, Thalia schooled Tarquin. She was maddened and aching at being eliminated. Her fault, not Tarquin's.

She rode Tarquin into the ring at a steady trot and cleared all the jumps from a controlled canter.

And then it was Sally.

"This isn't me," she thought. "Not me having to jump for first place!" The Haxton boy had gone clear, and if she was to be first, Willow must go clear as well.

As Sally cantered Willow in a circle, she heard the signal to start. Suddenly she was filled with the same confidence she had felt all day. She wasn't perched uneasily on the saddle but was sitting close to her horse, able to think and plan as she rode the course.

Willow cleared the first three jumps up the side of the ring and turned to take the diagonal row of jumps—a double, a brush, and a spread of poles. At the second part of the double Willow's timing was wrong and she had to stretch to clear it. Bending from her waist, her hands light on the reins, Sally went effortlessly with her horse.

They cleared the double and the brush, turned up the opposite side of the ring over two spreads and an upright, and were galloping back across the ring at the last jump—a high brick wall. Willow's hind foot clipped one of the bricks. It trembled but stayed in place. They were clear.

The team prizes were presented first. The cup went to the Haxton team. Then they called Sally's name as the individual winner.

"Well done, my dear," said the gray-haired man who was presenting the prizes. "Very well done indeed."

Sally took the cup and ribbon, stuttering over her thanks.

"Not only has this young lady won a cup for herself, but her dog saved a little boy from drowning. I'm happy to tell you that the child is now home in bed. But I think Sally Lorimer deserves another round of applause."

Sally sat numbly, staring into space as the burst of clapping swirled about her.

"Not me, this isn't me," Sally thought. But it was.

When at last the horses were loaded, Sally managed to escape from the congratulations, the praise, and the curious questions from Pony Club mothers who wanted to find out who she was. She climbed up into the cab of the horse trailer with Thalia and Martine, clutching her cup in both hands, still hardly able to believe her day.

They unloaded Buster and Zodiac at Ashdale and then drove on to Kestrel Manor. The vet was standing in Kestrel Manor's doorway.

"Oh, stop! Please stop!" cried Sally. "I must find out how Meg is."

Sally jumped down from the trailer, and to her utter delight, mattering far more than cups or ribbons, Meg came barking to meet her.

"She's all right," cried Sally, hugging Meg to her. "She's better? She's really better?"

"She's some dog," said the vet. "She's made it. Couldn't be better. I've seen them go on for years when these pills agree with them. She'll be on them for the rest of her days, but I don't suppose anyone will object to that."

"Can't thank you enough," said Mr. Lorimer, who had arrived home half an hour before Sally.

"Thank you," said Sally, stroking Meg's

head, feeling her alive and warm and well again. "Thank you very much."

"I told your dad," the vet said to Sally. "I was speaking to the dogcatcher about your hound. I stitched her up when the two men had her. No question of her being aggressive. She's one of the nicest-natured dogs I've known. Both men are off to work on the oil wells, so I expect they dumped her. Anyway, she's your dog now."

Even when they had seen to their horses and Willow had finished her feed and was pulling contentedly at her hay net, Sally could not bear to leave her. She wanted to stay with her, to relive in her mind the best day of her life.

"I'm starving," insisted Thalia. "Utterly empty. Come on."

Sally took one long, last look at Willow, her horse, who had galloped and jumped so boldly and yet taken her sweetly through the dressage test. The best horse.

"You do realize," said Thalia as they walked toward Kestrel Manor, "I am absolutely eaten up with jealousy. I'm concentrating on Tarquin's show jumping. Martine said she was incredulous.

And it does mean, now that you're completely not nervous, we can jump at the big shows Qualify for the Horse of the Year Show! Anything, absolutely anything!"

Suddenly Sally thought about her crystal unicorn. All day it had lain safely in her pocket.

Fen was lying on the doorstep. When she saw them coming, she uncoiled herself and—tail swinging, eyes bright—came to meet them, walking close to Sally's side.

Thalia pushed the kitchen door open and stood back. Sally found herself in a room full of people—all her family, Narg, Mrs. Blair and Verity, Simon and his father, Martine—and Misty and Meg. The long kitchen table was loaded with food, with pies and cakes and cookies. Sally stared in blank amazement.

Her father held up his glass.

"To the winner," he said, smiling proudly at her.

"Not me," said Sally. "It was all Willow. She's the winner."

Don't miss

Horseshoes
#5

Show Jumper Wanted

With the course she was to jump clear in her mind, Sally rode Willow at the first jump. Normally when Sally jumped, her mind was cold and clenched, but today was different. She was thinking about takeoffs and landings, about being ready for the next jump, about going fast for spreads and slower for height.

Willow, feeling her rider's determination, made nothing of the first three jumps. She cleared the double with neat-hoofed accuracy. When she had popped over the next two jumps, she was ready to turn and face the last jump— the red-and-white wall.

Suddenly Sally realized that the wall had been raised. "I must stop Willow from jumping," zipped through her mind. But only for a second. "Thalia would jump," she thought, and instantly she was riding Willow at the wall.

Willow checked, as she too realized the height of the wall.

"On you go," cried Sally, urging Willow on with seat and heels.

Willow rose in a perfect arc and landed far out. Sally, patting her neck and praising her horse, galloped on out of the indoor school with the applause of the invisible spectators filling her head.

"We did it," Sally cried. "No one made us. We did it ourselves." For a second she was overflowing with glory, before the thought of Thalia in the hospital and Tarquin stolen came back to her.